**COLLINGWOOD O'HARE ENTERTAINMENT LTD**

First published 2002 by Walker Books Ltd
87 Vauxhall Walk, London SE11 5HJ

2 4 6 8 10 9 7 5 3 1

Based on the animated series "Eddy & the Bear"
Series developed by Tony Collingwood and Helen Stroud
Produced by Christopher O'Hare

© 2002 Collingwood O'Hare Entertainment Ltd

Printed and bound in Great Britain by Ebenezer Bayliss Ltd

British Library Cataloguing in Publication Data:
a catalogue record for this book is available
from the British Library

ISBN 0-7445-8976-2

# Eddy & the Bear in

# The Latest Craze

From the original script by Jez Alborough

WALKER BOOKS
AND SUBSIDIARIES
LONDON • BOSTON • SYDNEY

On his way to school one sunny morning, Eddy went to see his friend Bear.

He ran through the field towards the wood. "Bear!" called Eddy. "Look what I've got!"

Bear waved hello. "You've got a box, Eddy!"

"No, silly!" said Eddy, laughing.
"Look what's *inside.*"

Bear leaned forward to take a closer look as Eddy opened the lid. Very gently, Eddy lifted out something heavy and grey with a funny painted face.

Bear sniffed at it suspiciously. "Is it a tortoise?"

Eddy laughed. "No, it's my new pet rock! His name's Boris. Everyone at school has one – it's the latest craze."

"Oh!" said Bear. "What does Boris do?"

"Pet rocks don't *do* anything," said Eddy. "You just look after them."

"Really?" said Bear. He'd never met a rock who needed looking after.

When Eddy had raced off to show Boris to his friends at school, Bear sat down to think. "I don't want to be left out of this 'craze' thing," he decided. "I'd better find my own pet rock straight away."

At school, Eddy got a surprise. The pet rock craze was already over! Instead, everyone had a yo-yo.

"I'd better start practising," said Eddy. There was a yo-yo in his old toy box, so he rushed home after school to look for it.

"Found it!" said Eddy.

Suddenly there was a huge *CRASH!* outside. Eddy ran to open the door. It was Bear, with a great big rock.

"H-h-hello, Eddy," panted Bear. "Meet my pet rock. He's called Hudson!"

"The pet rock craze finished *ages* ago, Bear," said Eddy. "This is what's cool now. It's called a yo-yo. You can help me practise."

But at school the next day, Eddy found out that all his practising had been a waste of time.

"Hey Eddy, can you play flick-bags?" asked his friend Harold.
"It's the latest craze!"

"No," said Eddy sadly.
"I was only just getting good at yo-yos."

Later, Eddy told Bear all about it.
"It's not fair. Just as I get used to something, the craze changes! First pet rocks, then yo-yos, now flick-bags – I can't keep up!"

"You're right. It's not fair," grumbled Bear. Then he got an idea. "I know! Why don't *we* start the next craze?"

"Yeah!" said Eddy. "That way we'll be really good at it before everyone else!"

"Exactly," said Bear.

"But what kind of craze?" asked Eddy.

"A silly one!" said Bear, taking a pair of big green pants from the clothes-line. "How about … the Wearing-Pants-on-Your-Head craze?"

"Yeah! *That* might catch on!" said Eddy, laughing. "Just imagine…"

"I like it," said Eddy with a giggle, "but maybe it's a bit too silly for the kids at school."

"Not too silly for me," said Bear. "I am a very silly bear, you know."

"Yes, you are silly – but that's what makes you so cool!" said Eddy.

And that's when Eddy got an even better idea.

The next morning, Bear walked into school with Eddy ... and took a seat in the classroom.

"Isn't your bear going home?" asked Harold.

"'Course not," replied Eddy. "Haven't you heard? Having a bear is the latest craze!"

Everyone thought it was such a cool idea that at lunch-time they all rushed home to collect bears of their own.

"We did it!" Eddy told Bear. "We started the bear craze."

"I know!" said Bear. He was so happy, he sang "I'm a craze, and I don't care – I'm a crazy, wibbly, wobbly bear!" – and everyone clapped along.

The very next morning, Bear ran all the way to school, excited to see Eddy and his friends again. But when he got there, something was missing.

"Where are all the bears?" he gasped.

"Sorry, Bear!" said Harold. "Rockets are the craze now!"

Behind Harold, Bear saw Eddy playing rockets with the other children.

"Then I guess Eddy won't need *me* any more," said Bear sadly.

Turning away, he trudged slowly home.

After school, Eddy found Bear in the woods looking very upset.

"I thought you wouldn't want to see me now that bears aren't the craze any more," said Bear.

"But Bear! You're not just a craze to me," said Eddy. "Crazes come and go, but you'll always be my best friend – for ever."

"Oh, good," said Bear, smiling. "'Cause I've been thinking about my pants idea. Is it really too silly?"

"Nothing's too silly for us," said Eddy.

"I know!" said Bear.

Eddy and Bear thought it was the best craze ever.

**Jez Alborough** says,

"Eddy & the Bear books are all about friendship. Wouldn't we all like to have a friend like Bear? One who is silly and fun, but also kind and loving. When you have a friend like that, everything you do together becomes an adventure. Each Eddy & the Bear book captures one of their adventures – so we can all join in!"

Jez Alborough has written and illustrated numerous children's picture books, including **Cuddly Dudley**, **Watch Out! Big Bro's Coming!**, **Hug** and the three original stories about Eddy and the Bear: **Where's My Teddy?**, **It's the Bear!** and **My Friend Bear**.

ISBN 0-7445-3058-X (pb)

ISBN 0-7445-4385-1 (pb)

ISBN 0-7445-6918-4 (pb)

Look out for more books based on the popular animated TV series Eddy & the Bear!